BROWNIE & PEARL

Step Out

by CYNTHIA RYLANT ✸ pictures by BRIAN BIGGS

Beach Lane Books
New York London Toronto Sydney

Look who's stepping out:
Brownie and Pearl!

They are going to a party.

It's a birthday party.

Cats are invited.

There's the house.
See all the balloons?

Now it's time to knock.

Uh-oh.

Brownie feels shy.
Maybe she'll go home.

But Pearl isn't shy.

Look!
Pearl went in
the kitty door!

Now Brownie *has* to knock.

Welcome to the party, Brownie!

Brownie likes the party.
She plays games.

She eats cake.
She eats ice cream.

She eats *more* ice cream.

Brownie is happy
that Pearl went in the kitty door.

Pearl is happy too!

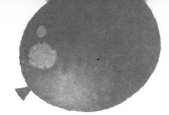

For Pascale
—C. R.

For Sacha, Harry, and Jake
—B. B.

BEACH LANE BOOKS
An imprint of Simon & Schuster Children's Publishing Division
1230 Avenue of the Americas, New York, New York 10020
Text copyright © 2010 by Cynthia Rylant
Illustrations copyright © 2010 by Brian Biggs
BEACH LANE BOOKS is a trademark of Simon & Schuster, Inc.
For information about special discounts for bulk purchases,
please contact Simon & Schuster Special Sales at 1-866-506-1949 or business@simonandschuster.com.
The Simon & Schuster Speakers Bureau can bring authors to your live event. For more information
or to book an event, contact the Simon & Schuster Speakers Bureau at 1-866-248-3049
or visit our website at www.simonspeakers.com.
Book design by Dan Potash and Sonia Chaghatzbanian
The text for this book is set in Berliner Grotesk.
The illustrations for this book are rendered digitally.
Manufactured in China
First Edition
2 4 6 8 10 9 7 5 3 1
Library of Congress Cataloging-in-Publication Data
Rylant, Cynthia.
Brownie & Pearl step out / Cynthia Rylant ; illustrated by Brian Biggs.—1st ed.
p. cm.
Summary: A little girl named Brownie arrives at a birthday party feeling shy
while her cat Pearl confidently enters through the "kitty door."
ISBN: 978-1-4169-8632-4
[1 Parties—Fiction. 2. Cats—Fiction.] I. Biggs, Brian, ill. II. Title.
III. Title: Brownie and Pearl step out.
PZ7.R982Bt 2010
[E]—dc22
2008032804